Best Friends Forever

Written by Christine Ricci

Louis Weber, C.E.O.
Publications International, Ltd.
7373 North Cicero Avenue, Lincolnwood, Illinois 60712
Ground Floor, 59 Gloucester Place, London W1U 8JJ

Customer Service: 1-800-595-8484 or customer_service@pilbooks.com

www.pilbooks.com

8 7 6 5 4 3 2 1

ISBN-13: 978-1-4127-8920-2
ISBN-10: 1-4127-8920-6

 publications international, ltd.

¡Hola! I'm Dora. This is Boots. We are best friends! *¡Buenos amigos!* What is your best friend's name? Best friends do lots of things together. Boots and I love to go exploring together, but we also like to read stories and play games together! What do you like to do with your best friend?

Best friends make each other feel special. I tell Boots that he's a super climber and he tells me that I'm great at soccer. What do you do to make your best friend feel special?

Best friends help each other.
Boots helps me find Explorer Stars and
I help Boots learn to speak Spanish.

And we both work together to stop Swiper from swiping!

Best friends take turns.
Sometimes I sit in front and
sled down the hill first, but
sometimes Boots sits in front
and I ride behind him.

Best friends share. I always share my orange slices with Boots and Boots always shares his cherries with me! That's why our picnics are so much fun! What do you share with your best friend?

Sometimes best friends hold hands. Boots and I like to hold hands. It makes us both feel better!

A best friend can make you laugh when you're feeling sad. Boots does triple back flips to make me laugh, and I tell jokes to make him laugh! We can be really silly! What silly things do you do with your best friend?

A best friend explores with you, plays with you, shares with you, laughs with you, and makes you feel special. I love my best friend, Boots!